ANNA ALTER

Francine's Day

Greenwillow Books
An Imprint of HarperCollins Publishers

For my mother

Francine's Day
Copyright © 2003 by Anna Alter
All rights reserved.
Manufactured in China.
www.harperchildrens.com

Pen-and-ink and watercolor paints
were used to prepare the full-color art.
The text type is Della Robbia.

Library of Congress Cataloging-in-Publication Data
Alter, Anna (date).
Francine's day / by Anna Alter.
    p.   cm.
"Greenwillow Books."
Summary: Francine the fox does not want
to go to school, but she has a good day anyway.
ISBN 0-06-623936-2 (trade).
ISBN 0-06-623937-0 (lib. bdg.)
[1. Schools—Fiction. 2. Kindergarten—Fiction.
3. Day—Fiction. 4. Foxes—Fiction.] I. Title.
PZ7.A4635 Fr 2003   [E]—dc21   2002033917

10 9 8 7 6 5 4 3 2 1
First Edition

Francine did not want to get out of bed.

But the teapot whistled,
and the dishes were clinking
in the kitchen.

Francine did not want
to take off her pajamas.

But the morning air was chilly,
and her warm fall clothes sat folded
on the rocking chair.

Francine did NOT want
to go to school today.

But her lunch was packed,
and the school bus was waiting
at the corner.

At school, Francine did not want to find her desk and say "Here" for roll call.

She did not want to sing
the "Good Morning" song,

and she did NOT want
to recite a poem in front
of the entire class.

Francine wanted a picnic at home with Mother. She wanted peanut butter sandwiches and apple juice cold from a thermos.

She did not want to sit at the snack table, but Mr. Wendell pulled out a chair and set her a place.

Francine wanted to make pictures
on her porch all afternoon. She
wanted crayons and sheets of
paper big enough to lie on top of.

She did not want to sit at the art table,
but Mr. Wendell poured out bright,
colored paint and handed her a brush.

Outside, the merry-go-round was spinning, the seesaw bounced up and down, and the swings sailed high into the air.

"I do not want to go to the playground," said Francine.

But Mr. Wendell said it would not be long until Mother met her at the bus stop.

That night, when it was time
to brush her teeth, Francine
recited a poem.
When it was time to put on
her pajamas, Francine was busy
singing a song to her friends.

She did not want to climb into bed.

But Mother pulled back
the covers, kissed her
good night, and turned off
the lights in her bedroom.

"It is time to close your
eyes and go to sleep,"
said Mother.

So she did.